Daniel's Pet

Alma Flor Ada

Illustrated by G. Brian Karas

Daniel held a small baby chick.

Daniel's Pet

Green Light Readers
Harcourt, Inc.
Orlando   Austin   New York   San Diego   London

It was soft in his hands.

"Can I have her as a pet?"
"Yes, Daniel," said Mama.

"I'll call her Jen," said Daniel.

Daniel fed Jen.

Daniel fed all the hens.

Daniel fed Jen every day.

Jen got very big.

One day, Daniel didn't see Jen.
"Jen! Jen!" Daniel called.

"Jen is in here," said Mama.
"Look at her eggs."

"Oh my!" said Daniel.
"Now I will have lots of pets!"

Think About It

1. **What is Daniel's pet?**

2. **What does Daniel's pet do?**

3. **Is Daniel surprised? How can you tell?**

4. **Why will Daniel have lots of pets now?**

5. **Would you like to have pets like Daniel's? Why or why not?**

Hatching an Egg

You can make one of Jen's new baby chicks!

WHAT YOU'LL NEED

- paper
- crayons or markers
- scissors
- tape

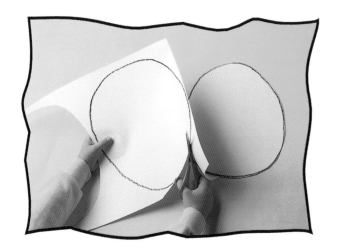

1. Cut out two egg shapes.

2. Draw a chick on one egg.

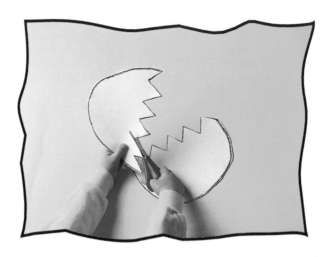

3. Cut the other egg in half.

4. Tape one half at the top
and the other half at
the bottom.

Use your hatching egg to tell a friend about Daniel, his pet chicken Jen, and Jen's new chicks!

Meet the Author and Illustrator

Alma Flor Ada has always loved to write about nature. As a child, she spent hours near a river watching plants, insects, birds, and frogs. Now she lives in a small house near a lake, where she still enjoys watching the natural world.

Brian Karas lives near many farms. He thought about the chickens he sees on those farms as he drew the pictures for *Daniel's Pet*.

To Cristina Isabel, who loves Daniel.
With love from Abuelita

—A. F. A.

For information about permission to reproduce selections from
this book, write to trade.permissions@hmhco.com or to Permissions,
Houghton Mifflin Harcourt Publishing Company, 3 Park Avenue,
19th Floor, New York, New York 10016.

www.hmhco.com

First Green Light Readers edition 2002
Green Light Readers is a trademark of Harcourt, Inc., registered in the
United States of America and/or other jurisdictions.

The Library of Congress has cataloged an earlier edition as follows:
Ada, Alma Flor.
Daniel's pet/Alma Flor Ada; illustrated by G. Brian Karas.
p. cm.
"Green Light Readers."
Summary: A young boy takes good care of his pet chicken, and
when she is grown up she gives him a surprise.
[1. Chickens—Fiction. 2. Pets—Fiction.] I. Karas, G. Brian, ill. II. Title.
PZ7.A1857Dap 2002
[E]—dc21   2001007732
ISBN 978-0-15-204825-9
ISBN 978-0-15-204865-5 (pb)

S C P   22 21 20 19 18 17 16
4 5 0 0 7 9 4 0 6 5
Printed in China

Ages 4-6
Grade: 1
Guided Reading Level: F-G
Reading Recovery Level: 10

Green Light Readers
For the reader who's ready to GO!

"A must-have for any family with a beginning reader."—*Boston Sunday Herald*

"You can't go wrong with adding several copies of these terrific books to your beginning-to-read collection."—*School Library Journal*

"A winner for the beginner."—*Booklist*

Five Tips to Help Your Child Become a Great Reader

1. Get involved. Reading aloud to and with your child is just as important as encouraging your child to read independently.

2. Be curious. Ask questions about what your child is reading.

3. Make reading fun. Allow your child to pick books on subjects that interest her or him.

4. Words are everywhere—not just in books. Practice reading signs, packages, and cereal boxes with your child.

5. Set a good example. Make sure your child sees YOU reading.

Why Green Light Readers Is the Best Series for Your New Reader

• Created exclusively for beginning readers by some of the biggest and brightest names in children's books

• Reinforces the reading skills your child is learning in school

• Encourages children to read—and finish—books by themselves

• Offers extra enrichment through fun, age-appropriate activities unique to each story

• Incorporates characteristics of the Reading Recovery program used by educators

• Developed with Harcourt School Publishers and credentialed educational consultants